W9-CPE-812

nickelodeon™

Story Time Collection

SpongeBob SquarePants created by

Stephen Hillenburg

randomhouse.com/kids

ISBN 978-0-385-38777-4

MANUFACTURED IN CHINA

10 9 8 7 6 5 4 3 2 1

nickelodeon™

Story Time Collection

Random House 🏠 New York

Contents

DORA SAVES THE ENCHANTED FOREST

Once upon a time, there was a magical land called the Enchanted Forest. King Unicornio, a kind and fair leader, ruled over the forest. All of the creatures there were free to do what they wanted to do. Honeybees could sing. Puppy dogs could try to fly. Oak trees could play hide-and-seek.

One sad day, everything changed. King Unicornio had to leave the Enchanted Forest. The kind and fair leader gave his crown to Owl and asked him to watch over the kingdom. But Owl was not kind and fair like Unicornio. He made new rules. He said that bees could not sing and dogs could not try to fly.

When Unicornio returned, Owl did not want to give the crown back. The sneaky bird led Unicornio into a trap! Owl had his mini-owls put a crack in the dam, and King Unicornio had to use his magic horn to plug the crack. If Unicornio didn't stay where he was, the Enchanted Forest would flood. So all of the creatures in the forest had to keep following Owl's unfair rules!

The creatures of the Enchanted Forest were not happy with Owl's rules. They wanted Unicornio to be their king, not Owl. They talked and talked. They knew there was only one person who could help them. Dora!

Do you see the way to get to the Enchanted Forest? Use your finger to show Dora the way to go.

Rabbit set out from the forest to look for her. He hopped through the Fairy Tunnel. He hopped past the Elf Garden. He hopped across the Cornfield. He found Dora and Boots jumping in the fall leaves outside of Dora's house.

"*¡Dora, Boots, vengan rápido!*" Rabbit called to his friends. "I know if you come, you can save the Enchanted Forest. We've got to rescue Unicornio so he can be king again!"

"We've got to find the quickest way to the Enchanted Forest," Dora answered. "Map can help us!"

Dora and Boots headed down the path to get to the Cornfield.
There they saw a scarecrow perched on his pole.

"¡Hola, Scarecrow!" Dora called. "Can we go through the
Cornfield, por favor?"

"We've got to rescue King Unicornio!"
Boots added.

Before the Scarecrow could answer,
Owl flew by.

He didn't want Dora to help Unicornio. He wanted to be king forever! He told the mini-owls to pile up lots and lots of corn. Dora and Boots could not get to the Enchanted Forest.

Scarecrow was happy to help Dora and Boots find a way to clear the path.

"Owl made a new rule," Scarecrow told them. "He said that scarecrows and crows can't go into the Enchanted Forest anymore."

"That's not fair!" Dora and Boots cried.

Dora watched as Scarecrow chased away four crows that were trying to pick up corn from the pile.

"If we invite the crows down, instead of chasing them away, they could clean up the path," she said to Scarecrow.

"Okay, I'll give it a try," Scarecrow replied. Scarecrow called out *"¡Bienvenidos, amigos!"* to the crows. That's how you say "Welcome, friends!" in Spanish.

Dora's plan worked like a charm. The crows picked up all of the corn. They cleared the path so Dora and Boots could head to their next stop—the Elf Garden!

"*¡Vámonos, Boots!*" Dora called. "Let's go!"

Dora and Boots raced down the path to the Elf Garden. Before they could get across the bridge that led to the garden, Owl flew by. He didn't want Dora to help Unicornio. He wanted to be king forever! He told the mini-owls to take the screws out of the bridge. Dora and Boots could not get to the Enchanted Forest.

The elves can fix the bridge if they work together. Will you work with them? Point to the pieces and show where they belong.

The elves were happy to help Dora and Boots find a way to fix the bridge.

"Owl made a new rule," the elves told them. "He said that elves can't go into the Enchanted Forest anymore."

"That's not fair!" Dora and Boots cried as they raced to the Fairy Tunnel.

Up ahead, the firefly fairies were shimmering around a patch of sunflowers. They collected light from the flowers to make their tails glow. Dora knew the fairies could use their light to show them the way through the dark tunnel.

Before they could get to the tunnel, Owl flew by. He didn't want Dora to help Unicornio. He wanted to be king forever! He told the mini-owls to blow out the fairies' lights. Dora and Boots could not get to the Enchanted Forest.

The little fairy still has her light. Will you make it grow? Rub your hands together to make more light!

The fairies were happy to help Dora and Boots find a way through the tunnel.

"Owl made a new rule," the elves told them. "He said that fairies can't go into the Enchanted Forest anymore."

"That's not fair!" Dora and Boots cried as they headed to the Enchanted Forest.

Dora and Boots were ready to rescue King Unicornio. They had made it across the Cornfield, past the Elf Garden, and through the Fairy Tunnel. There was just one thing left for them to do. They had to open the magic door that led to the Enchanted Forest.

Can you say the magic words to open the door? *¡Puerta mágica!* That means "magic door." Say *"¡Puerta mágica!"*

After they crossed through the magic door, Dora and Boots were sad to see how much the Enchanted Forest had changed. There were no scarecrows in the forest. There were no elves in the forest. There were no fairies in the forest. Owl even told the squirrels that they weren't allowed in the Enchanted Forest anymore!

Rabbit came hopping over to Dora and Boots.

"I'll take you to Unicornio, quick," he whispered to them. "He's protecting the forest with his horn."

"We've got to help him!" Dora agreed as she followed Rabbit.

Before they could get to the dam, Owl flew by. He didn't want Dora to help Unicornio. He wanted to be king forever! He told the mini-owls to make more leaks. Dora and Boots had to stay to plug the dam, too!

Dora looked over at the kind and fair Unicornio. He was so brave and loyal. He was not just a great leader, he was a good friend, too.

"Good friends, that's it!" Dora cried. "We made lots of friends today. Maybe they can help us one more time."

Dora and Boots thought about the friends they met on their way to the Enchanted Forest. The elves were really good at fixing things, so Dora sent Rabbit to go get them.

"Tell the elves to bring their tools!" she called to Rabbit as he hopped away. *"¡Rápido!"*

Quick as a flash, the elves came with their tools. They were eager to help fix the dam so that Unicornio could return to the Enchanted Forest.

Once the dam was all fixed up, it was time for the friends to head back into the Enchanted Forest and get Unicornio's crown back.

All of the creatures wanted Owl to leave the forest. But that was not fair either. The Enchanted Forest was for everyone!

"Owl, you are very smart, but you must learn to get along with others and treat everyone fairly," Unicornio told him. "I want you to do a service for everyone in the forest."

Owl was told to invite everyone to the biggest party the Enchanted Forest has ever seen. Then Owl returned the crown to King Unicornio. All of the creatures celebrated King Unicornio's return to the throne. They danced and sang as fireworks flashed in the sky.

¡Viva el rey Unicornio! Long live King Unicornio!

THE END

¡*H*ola! I'm Dora. Today I'm reading a special story called *The Crystal Kingdom* to my friend Boots. Do you want to hear it, too? Great!

Once upon a time, there were four crystals that helped light the Crystal Kingdom. The yellow crystal made the sun shine yellow. The blue one made the sky and ocean blue.

The green one made the grass and trees green. And
the red crystal joined the other colors to make a beautiful
rainbow! The townspeople loved their colorful world.

But the king did not like sharing the crystals. "Mine, mine, mine!" said the greedy king. He used his magic wand and took all of the crystals for himself. Without the crystals, the town lost all its wonderful color! But the king would not return the crystals. Instead he hid them in other stories where no one could find them!

A brave girl named Allie wanted to rescue the crystals.
She searched all over, but they were nowhere to be found.
Look! My crystal necklace is flashing! It's shining a
rainbow into the kingdom where Allie lives!

Allie is flying out of her story and into our forest! She needs our help! The Snow Princess says my magic crystal will shine only if there's still color in Allie's kingdom. We have to help Allie find the crystals to keep her home shining! Will you help us, too? *¡Fantástico!*

Hmmm . . . how will we find the crystals? Let's ask Map! Say "Map!" Map says the yellow crystal is in *The Dragon Land Story*, the green one is in *The Butterfly Cave Story*, the blue one is in *The Magic Castle Story*, and the red crystal is in *The Crystal Kingdom Story*! We've got to jump into my storybook to get all the crystals! Say *"¡La primera historia!"* to get us into the first story.

¡Muy bien! It worked! There are lots of dragons here. We
must be in *The Dragon Land Story*. The Snow Princess has
another message for us. She says that to find the yellow crystal,
we must save a fighting knight. *¡Vámonos!* Let's go!

There's a knight fighting a dragon! But that's a friendly dragon! We need to lasso the sword away from the knight. Backpack has a rope we can use to lasso the sword. Say "lasso" to help me lasso the sword! Good job!

The knight and dragon are happy that they stopped fighting. And the dragon knows where the yellow crystal is hidden! He saw the king put it inside a cliff. *Wheeee!* Let's fly the dragon to the yellow crystal!

Whoosh! The dragon is using his fire to blast open the cliff! We see the yellow crystal! But so does the king! He wants to steal the crystal, but the knight raises her shield and blocks his spell! Yay! We all worked together to get the yellow crystal. And the knight is giving us her shield to help us with the rest of our journey! Thanks, Knight!

Next we need to find the green crystal in *The Butterfly Cave Story.* Say *"¡La segunda historia!"* to get us into the second story.

We're here in *The Butterfly Cave Story*! Uh-oh! My crystal is losing color. That means color is fading from the kingdom. We've got to get that green crystal fast! Do you see the Butterfly Cave? *¡Vámonos!*

There's a caterpillar, and she's stuck! The Snow Princess says we can save her by shining sun into the cave. What do we have that's shiny? *¡Sí!* The shield! The sunlight is helping the caterpillar turn into a butterfly. *¡Una mariposa!* Now she can take us to the crystal!

The green crystal is inside the twelfth cocoon. Will you help us count to twelve to find it? One, two, three, four, five, six, seven, eight, nine, ten, eleven, twelve. Great! We found the green crystal. Oooh! The butterflies are hatching from the cocoons. And they're giving us each a pair of magic butterfly wings to help us on our adventure! *¡Muchas gracias!*

Now we've got to find the blue crystal in *The Magic Castle Story.* Say *"¡La tercera historia!"* to get into the third story! *¡Muy bien!*

We made it into *The Magic Castle Story*. There's someone here who can help us! His name is Enrique, and he's a magician.

The king took Enrique's bunnies from his magic hat and put the crystal inside it. Then he locked Enrique out of the castle! We need to find five of Enrique's lost bunnies. Do you see them? Good job!

We used our butterfly wings to fly up through a castle
window! To get the crystal out of the magic hat, we have to say
"Abracadabra!" Say "Abracadabra!" Yay! Allie has the yellow,
green, and blue crystals now. Enrique gives us his magic wand
to help on our adventure. *¡Gracias, Enrique!*

All we need is the red crystal to save the Crystal Kingdom!
To get us into the fourth story, say *"¡La cuarta historia!"*

We're in Allie's kingdom, but it's still losing color! And so is my necklace! The Snow Princess says that we have to use what we learned to get the red crystal from the king.

The greedy king has the crystal in his crown! What can we use to fly up to him? Right! Our butterfly wings! Whoa! Rocks are coming right at us! What can use to block the rocks? Yeah, the shield!

The king does not want to share his crystals. He's trying to take them from Allie with his magic wand! To break the king's spell with our magic wand, we need to say "Share!" Say "Share!" Yay! It worked! We got the red crystal!

The color is coming back to Crystal Kingdom! We
did it! The king is surprised that we are sharing the
crystals. He sees that everyone is happy, and he wants to
be happy too. Wow! The king gives Allie his crown and
makes her the queen! *¡La reina!*

The town is throwing a party to celebrate the return
of the crystals! The king is so happy that he learned how
to share. Thanks for helping us save Crystal Kingdom!
We couldn't have done it without all our brave friends . . .
especially you.

One afternoon, Dora was reading one of her favorite books, *Alice in Wonderland*, to Boots and Abuela's three kitties. It was about a girl named Alice who discovered a magical land.

Suddenly, there was a knocking sound from inside Dora's mirror! The mirror began to sparkle. The kitties ran to it and magically jumped inside!

Dora and Boots looked into the mirror and saw the kitties chasing a white rabbit. "We've got to hurry! The Queen is waiting!" called the rabbit.

"Dora, we have to get the kitties back!" cried Boots.

"If the kitties went through the mirror, maybe we can, too!" said Dora.

Dora and Boots pressed against the mirror—and tumbled through to the other side!

Dora and Boots found themselves in a strange, colorful world. Their clothes had magically changed!

"Dora, you look like Alice in Wonderland!" Boots said. Then he pointed to some rocks with legs. "And look! Those rocks are skipping!"

"We must be in Wonderland!" said Dora.

In the distance, Dora and Boots saw the kitties chasing the rabbit. The rabbit was carrying a tray of tarts.

"I've got to drop off all these tarts for the Queen's Tea Party!" he exclaimed. He disappeared down a tiny rabbit hole. The kitties followed close behind.

Dora and Boots were too big to fit through the rabbit hole. "We need to find another way to get to the Queen's Tea Party," said Dora. "Let's ask Map!"

"To get to the Queen's Tea Party, we need to sail to the Giant Trees, go past the Tiny Animals, and walk through the Forgetful Forest," said Map.

Dora and Boots followed Map's path to a wide ocean. The Giant Trees were on the other side. "We need a boat," said Dora. "Hey, maybe that guy in the hat can help us!" said Boots. It was the Mad Hatter!

"Do you have a boat that can take us to the Giant Trees?" Boots asked the Mad Hatter.

"No, but I have a hat!" the Hatter said. The Hatter took his hat off and threw it into the water. The hat grew to the size of a boat!

"C'mon, amigos. Hop into my hat!" said the Hatter. Dora and Boots climbed in, and they sailed to the Giant Trees.

Dora and Boots thanked the Mad Hatter and went into the Giant Forest. Giant birds flew overhead. Giant chipmunks and squirrels ran across the forest floor. A giant frog croaked.

"How are we going to get past all these giant animals?" asked Boots.

"You can swing on us!" said the Giant Trees. They let down two vines.
"Put your hands up and reach, reach, reach!" said Dora.
The two explorers reached high and grabbed the vines. They swung through the forest and past the giant animals!

As they continued on their way, Dora and Boots met Tweedledee and Tweedledum. They looked like a tiny Tico and a tiny Benny!

Tweedledee and Tweedledum heard that Dora was going to the Queen's Tea Party.

"You're gonna have to get past the Tiny Animals. But you've got to be careful because you're so big!" warned Tweedledum.

Soon Dora and Boots met a group of tiny cows, chickens, and pigs. Dora and Boots had found the Tiny Animals—and they were blocking the path!

"How will we get past?" asked Boots.

"We need to ask them politely to step aside. In Spanish, we say, *¡Con permiso!*'" replied Dora.

"*¡Con permiso!*" the two friends said to the Tiny Animals.

The Tiny Animals danced off the path. Dora and Boots thanked the animals and went on their way.

As they approached the Forgetful Forest, a large, fluffy cat suddenly appeared. It was the Cheshire Cat!

The Cheshire Cat gave Dora and Boots some advice. "In the Forgetful Forest, you can forget all kinds of things. It's important to remember who you are, what you want, and where you're going."

As they walked through the Forgetful Forest, Dora and Boots repeated who they were, what they wanted, and where they were going so they wouldn't forget. They had nearly made it through when they came to a door.

"I've got this," Boots told Dora. He turned to the door. "She's Dora, and I'm Boots. We're looking for the kitties, and we're going to the Queen's Tea Party."

The door swung open. Boots had done it!

Dora and Boots went though the door and found the Queen's Tea Party. Their Wonderland friends were there, including the rabbit with the Queen's tarts—and the kitties!

Everyone wanted tarts, but the mean Queen did not want to share.

Just then, the Knave of Hearts appeared. He looked just like Swiper! The sneaky fox wanted to steal the Queen's tarts!

The Queen pointed to everyone else. "Take *their* things! But leave my tarts alone."

To protect her Wonderland friends, Dora held up her hand. "Swiper, no swiping!" she said.

"Oh, mannn!" said Swiper.

"Dora stopped the Knave of Hearts!" cried the rabbit. "She protected us. She should be Queen!"

The Mad Hatter pulled a crown from his hat. He put it on Dora. The crown turned Dora's dress into a sparkling gown!

"Queen Dora! *¡La reina Dora!*" everyone cheered.

Dora shook her head. "I'm really honored, but I'm not a queen. I'm Dora, and I need to bring Abuela's kitties back home."

The Queen looked sad. "Everyone wants you as Queen because you're so brave."

"I always have help," Dora told the Queen. "Today the Cheshire Cat helped us. So did Tweedledum and Tweedledee. And we wouldn't have gotten anywhere without the Mad Hatter!"

"How can I be a better Queen?" asked the Queen.

Dora turned to the Mad Hatter. "The Queen wants to change. Can you help her?"

"She's gonna need a new hat!" said the Mad Hatter.

Dora gave the Queen her crown. When she put it on, her gown magically changed!

"I feel so much better!" said the Queen. "I'm going to need your help," she told the rabbit. "Bring your tarts. Pass them out to everyone!"

After the party, Dora and Boots returned home with Abuela's kitties. "We did it!" said Boots. "We made it to the Queen's Tea Party, and we got the kitties back! And we got the Queen to be nice and share!"

Dora poured Boots and the kitties some tea. "What a wonderful adventure in Wonderland!" she said.

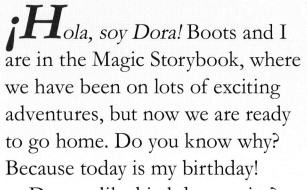

¡Hola, soy Dora! Boots and I are in the Magic Storybook, where we have been on lots of exciting adventures, but now we are ready to go home. Do you know why? Because today is my birthday!

Do you like birthday parties? Me too! My friends and family are having a birthday party for me! Will you come to my birthday party? *¡Fantástico!* I can't wait to go back home for the party!

Oh, no! A twisty wind cloud is carrying us away.
It looks like we are headed to another part of the
Magic Storybook! Hold on, Boots!

The twisty wind cloud blew us all the way to Wizzle World. But that's okay. All we have to do is jump out of the Magic Storybook and we'll be back in the rainforest in no time. Ready? Let's jump!

Hmm. Jumping out of the storybook isn't working. Boots and I are still in Wizzle World. The Wizzles want to help us. They remember Boots and me because we helped them before. The Wizzles tell us that the only way to get home from Wizzle World is if the Wishing Wizzle wishes us home. But the Wishing Wizzle can't make any more wishes because he doesn't have his wishing crystal!

¡Mira! I have a crystal! The Wizzles tell me that this is the wishing crystal. Now we just need to get it to the Wishing Wizzle so he can wish us back to the rainforest! *¡Vámonos!* Let's go!

The Wizzles warn us to be careful of La Bruja, the Mean Witch. She doesn't like wishes. She's the one who took the Wishing Wizzle's wishing crystal so he couldn't make any more wishes.

We're off to see the Wishing Wizzle! But where is he? Who do we ask for help when we don't know which way to go? Yeah, Map!

Map says to get to the Wishing Wizzle, we go across the Sea Snake Lake, then through the Dancing Forest, and then over the Rainbow. Then we'll reach the Wishing Wizzle, and he can wish us back home for my birthday party!

We made it to Sea Snake Lake, and I see a big, big snake! How will we get across the lake? I know—that bubble can carry us across the lake above the sea snake!

Look! It's La Bruja, the Mean Witch. She's zapping our bubble and popping holes in it! This is not good!

My crystal is lighting up—the Snow Princess has a message for us. She says we'll need the help of our friends to get past La Bruja. If we need help, we can ask the crystal to remember our friends. Say *"¡Recuerda a mis amigos!"*

The crystal shows us a time when Benny had a hole in his hot-air balloon. Remember how we brought Benny sticky tape to fix his balloon? We can also use sticky tape to patch up the holes in the bubble. I have some sticky tape in my Backpack. Say "Backpack!"

Do you see the sticky tape? Smart looking!

We have to tape up the holes quickly. But first we need to count the holes. Count with me! 1, 2, 3, 4, 5, 6, 7, 8, 9, 10, 11. Eleven holes.

Good counting! Now let's tape them up.

Yay! We made it past Sea Snake Lake. So next is the Dancing Forest. But first we need to go through this field of flowers.

Look! One of the flowers has Boots's tail! We need to help Boots. The snappy flowers speak Spanish, so we need to help Boots say "open" in Spanish. Say *"¡Abre, por favor!"* Open, please!

You did it! Thanks for helping Boots!

We're at the entrance to the Dancing Forest, but the trees aren't dancing. La Bruja put a spell on the trees that made them stop dancing—and now they're trying to stop us from getting through the forest!

We need to ask the crystal to remember our friends! Say *"¡Recuerda a mis amigos!"* Remember how we helped the Pirate Piggies dance past the Coconut Conga trees? I bet if we danced the Coconut Conga, the trees will want to dance and they'll have to let us go through. Let's wiggle, wiggle, wiggle!

Great job! We made it through the Dancing Forest. Where do we go next? The Rainbow! Yeah! *El arco iris.* Thanks for helping. We just need to follow this path to the Rainbow. Let's go!

Uh-oh. The path stopped. How are we going to get
to the Rainbow? Maybe that scarecrow knows the way.

The scarecrow is crying. He says that the crows keep scaring him, even though it's his job to scare the crows away. The scarecrow says he will lead us to the Rainbow if we can show him how to scare the crows away. That's easy. To scare crows away, all you have to say is "Boo!" Say it with us: "Boo!"

We did it! Good job!

The scarecrow points us in the direction of the Rainbow.
Thanks, scarecrow! We have to travel over the Rainbow to get to
the Wishing Wizzle. Do you see someone who can take us there?
A unicorn! Smart looking!

Oh, no! La Bruja made it rain, and the Rainbow is disappearing! We need help—and fast. Tell the crystal *"¡Recuerda a mis amigos!"* Remember our friends! Look at the crystal! Our friends are singing, *"Rain, rain, go away! Come again another day!"* Sing with us!

It's working! The Rainbow is coming back!

We made it over the Rainbow. *¡Gracias, Unicornio!* And there's the Wishing Wizzle. He's so happy to see that we brought him his crystal— now he can grant wishes again! And he can wish us home for my birthday!

Oh, no! La Bruja has cracked the crystal with her bolts of lightning. The Wishing Wizzle says that the wishing crystal has lost its power, but there might be one way to make it work again. The Wishing Wizzle says I will need all of my friends to help. Everyone has to wish really hard. They have to say "I wish Dora back home."

Our friends are wishing us home! But the Wishing Wizzle says the crystal needs more power. There's just one friend who's missing—it's you! Will you wish us back home? Say "I wish Dora back home!"

It worked! We made it home for my party! We couldn't have done it without help from our friends—and you! Thank you for helping Boots and me get back home for my party. This is the best birthday ever!

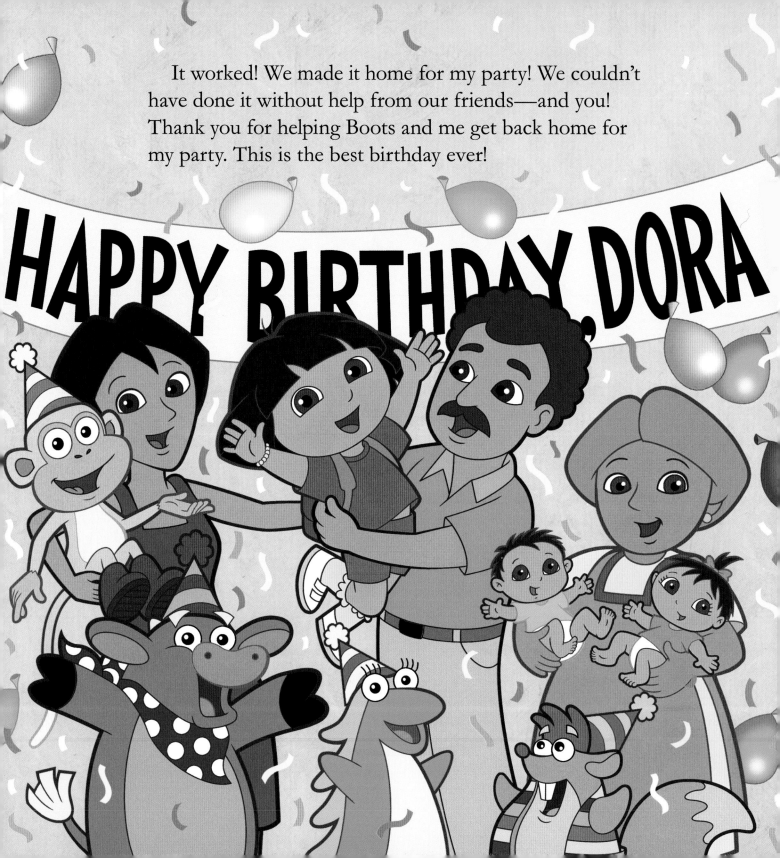

HAPPY BIRTHDAY, DORA

103

Early one morning, Molly and Gil were on their way to school with Bubble Puppy. Suddenly, a squirrel jumped out of the bushes.

"*Arf! Arf!*" barked Bubble Puppy. He ran after the squirrel and chased it up a tree. But then he couldn't get down!

Gil climbed up to help Bubble Puppy. When he looked down, he got really dizzy. Gil was stuck, too!

A fire truck raced over to the tree, and a firefighter got out. He called to his partner to raise the ladder, and then he climbed up and rescued Gil and Bubble Puppy!

"Thanks for saving us!" Gil said to the
firefighter. Bubble Puppy barked happily. Gil
noticed that the firefighter had a dog, too.
"This is Dotty. She's our fire
dog!" said the firefighter.

After the fire truck left, Molly, Gil, and Bubble Puppy
continued on their way to school.

"I can't wait to tell everyone about getting rescued by
a real firefighter!" said Gil.

In the classroom, Gil and Molly told Mr. Grouper and their friends about their adventure. "I just got rescued by a firefighter! Bubble Puppy and I were stuck in a tree, and he saved us!" Gil said.

"Yeah!" said Molly. "He raised the ladder and climbed way up high to help!"

"Sounds like a real emergency!" exclaimed Mr. Grouper.
"What's an emergency?" Oona asked.
"An emergency is when someone needs help right away," answered Nonny.

Gil thought the firefighter was totally awesome.
He wanted to be a firefighter, too! "What does a
firefighter do?" he asked Mr. Grouper.

"Let's find out," said Mr. Grouper. "Line up,
everybody! We're going to the fire station!"
"Field trip!" the Bubble Guppies cheered.

When the Bubble Guppies and Mr. Grouper arrived at the fire station, they saw a fire truck outside. It had a long ladder and a shiny siren.

"A fire truck has everything you need in an emergency,"
Mr. Grouper explained as everyone gathered around.
"Let's take a look!"

"When firefighters get to an emergency, they might need to rescue someone way up high. That means they'll have to climb a ladder," said Mr. Grouper.

Gil and Molly watched as a firefighter raised the long ladder into the air.

"And if firefighters have to put out a fire, they use a hose," continued Mr. Grouper.

A firefighter attached a hose to a fire hydrant, and water gushed out.

"When there's an emergency, a fire truck turns on its siren. The bright lights and loud sound tell everyone to move out of the way so the firefighters can do their job," Mr. Grouper explained.

The Bubble Guppies started home from the station. "Firefighters are the coolest! I want to be a firefighter!" exclaimed Gil.

Just then, they saw a fire truck on the road with its lights flashing. The siren blared. There was an emergency!

Gil and Molly followed the fire truck to the emergency. Dotty and some firefighters were stuck! Dotty had chased a squirrel into a tree. When the firefighters tried to rescue her, their ladder had broken.

"This is a job for
Firefighter Gil!" Gil said.

Gil went into the fire truck
and put on a fire hat and coat. He
bravely climbed up the ladder. But
it wasn't long enough! Gil pulled a
walkie-talkie out of his coat. "We
need to make the ladder taller!" he
told Molly.

Molly nodded and
pulled the lever that raised
the ladder.

The ladder got taller and taller. Putting one hand over the other, Gil climbed the last few rungs—and reached the firefighters and Dotty! Gil had saved the day!

They all climbed down the ladder
until they were safely on the ground.
"*Arf! Arf!*" barked Dotty.
"She's saying thank you,"
a firefighter told Gil with a smile.

125

"Hooray for Firefighter Gil!" everyone cheered.

DUMP TRUCK TROUBLE

One sunny morning, Gil and Goby were playing in the park. "Vroom! Vroom!" rumbled Goby as he pushed his dump truck. Gil dug through the sand with his bulldozer. Suddenly, he heard honking sounds coming from the other side of a big fence! "Whoa!" he said. "Check this out, Goby!"

"It's a construction site!" Goby exclaimed. "Look—there's a dump truck! And a bulldozer! And a crane!"

Gil and Goby wanted to share their discovery with the rest of the Bubble Guppies. They raced to school.

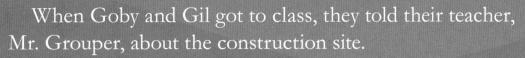

When Goby and Gil got to class, they told their teacher, Mr. Grouper, about the construction site.

"There was a bulldozer just like mine!" said Gil, holding up his toy.

"And there was a dump truck just like— Oh, no! I forgot my dump truck!" Goby cried.

Mr. Grouper led the Bubble Guppies
back to the construction site. Goby's
dump truck was nowhere to be found!
"Let's go ask if anyone has seen your
dump truck," suggested Gil.

"Excuse me," Mr. Grouper called to one of the construction workers. "Have you seen a toy dump truck around here?"

"No, I'm sorry, I haven't," a construction worker named Liz replied. "But I'll sure keep an eye out for it."

"Construction vehicles are cool," said Nonny.

"What does 'vehicle' mean?" asked Oona.

"A vehicle is something that carries or moves things," replied Nonny.

"There are many different kinds of construction vehicles," explained Mr. Grouper. "The one that pushes piles of dirt and rocks is called a bulldozer. Dump trucks carry stuff, and the really tall one that lifts things high into the air is called a crane."

The Bubble Guppies returned to school, talking excitedly about construction vehicles.

Back in class, Goby couldn't stop worrying about his toy dump truck. So later that day, Mr. Grouper took the Guppies on a field trip to look for Goby's toy.

When they arrived, the construction site had become a rodeo!

Liz the construction worker was now the rodeo's announcer.
"Welcome to the Bubbletucky Construction Rodeo!" she said.
"Excuse me. Did you find my friend's dump truck?" asked Gil.
"Nobody's been able to find it," Liz replied sadly. "But you
boys go enjoy the rodeo, and afterward, we'll see what we can do."

The Bubble Guppies watched dump trucks, bulldozers, and cranes zoom around the rodeo ring. For the big finale, three dump trucks dumped sand into big piles in front of three holes in the ground.

"Get ready for El Dozer!" Liz announced. "He is going to put those piles of sand into those holes!"

As El Dozer bulldozed the sand piles into the holes, Gil and Goby noticed a toy dump truck sticking out of the third hole.

"Stop the rodeo!" shouted Gil. "Goby's dump truck—it's down there!"

Liz leapt up. "Come with me!" she called.

With Gil and Goby close behind, Liz climbed into the rodeo ring. She jumped into a crane. Just before El Dozer pushed the third sand pile into the last hole, Liz lowered the crane claw and scooped up Goby's toy dump truck!

"Thank you for saving my truck!" Goby said to Liz.
"You're welcome!" she replied.
Soon Gil and Goby were back in the sand. Goby pushed
his dump truck over a hill. "Dump truck coming through!"
he said happily.

LET'S BUILD A DOGHOUSE!

One day, Gil was playing fetch with Bubble Puppy.

"Hey, Gil! How's it going?" Molly asked.

"Great!" replied Gil. "But I have a big project to do today. I want to build Bubble Puppy a doghouse."

"Remember that construction site we visited? Maybe we can ask some construction workers for help!" Molly suggested.

At the construction site, Gil and Molly met some construction workers. They wore bright yellow vests and hard hats.

"Will you help us build a doghouse for Bubble Puppy?" Gil asked.

"Of course!" said the construction workers.

First the workers drew a plan for Bubble Puppy's doghouse. "This is called a blueprint," one of them explained.

Once the blueprint was finished, the workers told Gil and Molly that they needed to go to the hardware store for supplies.

Gil and Molly went to Deema and Goby's hardware store, where they found all the supplies they needed to build Bubble Puppy's doghouse.

Nails

"Don't forget the paint!" said Deema, handing them a bucket.
"And your tools!" added Goby, pointing to a tool board.

PAINT

It was time to start! Molly and Oona held a piece of wood while a worker sawed through it. He cut the wood into boards of the same length.

Gil and Molly invited the rest of the Bubble Guppies and Mr. Grouper to the construction site to help build Bubble Puppy's doghouse. When they arrived, all the Bubble Guppies put on hard hats to be safe.

A construction worker showed Oona and Gil the plan for the doghouse. "Before we start, we check the blueprint to make sure we've planned everything right," he said.

To build the top of the doghouse, a construction worker cut boards into different sizes. Then he put them together to make a triangle frame.

Using wrenches, Goby and the worker bolted the boards together.

Then Mr. Grouper hammered nails into the boards. When he was done, he had made one side of Bubble Puppy's doghouse!

Working together, the Bubble Guppies, Mr. Grouper,
and the construction workers built a *fin*-tastic doghouse
for Bubble Puppy! On top, they built a balcony with a little
horn to toot. There was even a slide that wrapped around
the house and ended at a pool at the bottom!

After they
were done, Molly
and Gil showed
Bubble Puppy the
doghouse. "What
do you think of
your new home?"
they asked him.

Bubble Puppy swam up to the top of his home
and tooted the horn. *"Arf! Arf!"* he barked.

Gil beamed. "Bubble Puppy loves his new doghouse!" he exclaimed.

"This is the best doghouse ever!" said Gil.
"Arf! Arf!" Bubble Puppy agreed.

BUBBLE GUPPIES

A FRIEND AT THE ZOO!

One beautiful summer day, Gil and Molly were playing with a flying disc. As Molly threw the disc to Gil, a gust of wind carried it over a high wall.

So Gil and Molly went to get it back.

On the other side of the wall, they found a zoo! Gil and Molly saw their disc next to the zookeeper. The zookeeper was feeding a large animal with a horn on its nose.

"Meet Monty the Rhino," said the zookeeper.
"He looks kinda sad," said Gil.
The zookeeper nodded. "I think Monty's a little lonely.
He could use a friend."

"I'll be his friend!" said Gil.

"Me too!" said Molly.

The zookeeper smiled. "Thank you so much. But I think Monty needs a friend that can live with him at the zoo."

Gil and Molly said goodbye to Monty and the zookeeper and headed to school.

"I'm gonna find a friend for Monty that can live at the zoo," said Gil.

Molly smiled. "Good idea! Let's go tell Mr. Grouper!"

Molly and Gil swam to class. Together with Goby, Deema, Oona, and Nonny, they greeted their teacher. "Good morning, Mr. Grouper!"

"Good morning, class!" Mr. Grouper replied.

"Gil and I saw a lonely rhino named Monty at the zoo,"
said Molly. "Mr. Grouper, will you help us find him a friend?"
"Sure!" replied Mr. Grouper. "Let's go to the zoo and find
a friend for Monty. Line up, everybody!"

At the zoo, the Bubble Guppies saw many animals in their habitats. "A habitat is a place where an animal lives," said Nonny. The animals lived in lots of different habitats. Monkeys swung from vines in the jungle. A panda climbed over his bamboo house. The penguins stayed nice and cool in their icy igloo.

Nonny pointed to a sign with a picture of a bird on the horn of a rhino. "Look," he said. "This bird and the rhino are friends."

"Maybe Monty should have a bird friend!" said Gil.

"That's a great idea!" said the zookeeper.

"We have lots of birds at the zoo!" said the zookeeper. "We just have to find a bird who can live in the same habitat as Monty."

The zookeeper pointed to a penguin. "Do you think a penguin would be a good friend?"

"No. A penguin needs a cold place to live, and Monty lives in a warm place!" said Molly.

"What about a macaw?" asked the zookeeper. "He lives in a tropical forest, where it's warm."

Gil shook his head. "A macaw lives high up in the trees, but rhinos live in flat, grassy plains. He wouldn't make a good friend for Monty."

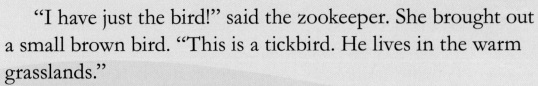

"I have just the bird!" said the zookeeper. She brought out a small brown bird. "This is a tickbird. He lives in the warm grasslands."

"Just like Monty!" said Molly.

"It's like the bird from the sign," said Gil. "A tickbird is the perfect bird friend for Monty!"

"Monty, meet your new friend!" said the zookeeper.
The tickbird flew over and landed on Monty's horn.
Monty started to smile.
"Hooray!" cheered the Bubble Guppies.

173

"Thanks for visiting the zoo today," the zookeeper told
Molly and Gil.

Molly laughed. "It was wonderful! We learned so much about
animals—and we found the perfect friend for Monty!"

TEAM
UMIZOOMI

Legend
of the
Blue Mermaid

One sunny day, Team Umizoomi was visiting the Umi City Beach. There were lots of things to see by the ocean!

"I see a sailboat!" said Milli.

"I see some sea lions!" said Geo.

What do you see?

"Look over there!" said Milli. "It's a mermaid statue!"

"This is a statue of the Blue Mermaid," said Bot. "Let's check my Super Robot Computer to find out more about her!"

The Blue Mermaid lived in the sea. She had a lot of friends:
2 dolphins, 3 turtles, 4 fish, and sea horses!

Count the sea horses.

Everyone in the sea loved the Blue Mermaid. But the most amazing thing about her was her tail. It was covered with sparkly blue scales! They were so bright, they lit up the ocean.

One day, Squiddy the Squid saw the tail.

"It makes the most beautiful light!" he said. He wanted to have the light all to himself. He made a special trap and captured the Blue Mermaid. No one could find her.

181

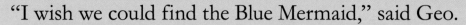

"I wish we could find the Blue Mermaid," said Geo.
"If only we knew where Squiddy took her!" said Milli.
"Look!" said Bot. "There's a bottle. And there's a note inside."

Who is the note from?

The note was from the Blue Mermaid! She was trapped in Squiddy's secret sand castle.

The Blue Mermaid sent out a trail of sparkly blue scales.

"We have to follow them to save her!" said Milli.

"Team Umizoomi, it's time for action!"
The trail of sparkly blue scales went across the ocean.
Team Umizoomi needed a boat.
"I can build a sailboat with a triangle, a rectangle, and
a semicircle," said Geo. *Super Shapes!*

"Nice sailboat, Geo!" Bot said. "Life jackets on! Let's go!"

Team Umizoomi followed the sparkly blue scales.
"Not so fast, Team Umizoomi!" It was Squiddy! He had
a wave machine. He used it to make a big wave.

What
number is
on the wave?

"The wave is a seven! We need to shrink it down to a one.
Let's count down from seven!" said Milli.
7, 6, 5, 4, 3, 2, 1!

"Let's keep following the scales!" said Bot.

How many sparkly blue scales do you see?

"Look!" said Geo. "The mermaid's trail goes onto that beach."

"Not so fast, Team Umizoomi!" It was Squiddy!

"I booby-trapped every shape on this island! Except for the triangles."

"If we only step on triangles," Geo said, "we can get to the other side. We need your help!"

Point to the triangles!

"We made it!" said Milli. "Great job, team!"
"Thanks for leading the way, Geo," said Bot.
Then the trail of sparkly blue scales went under
the water. "Scuba gear on!"

192

Team Umizoomi followed the scales under the sea. They found Squiddy's secret sand castle!

"There's the Blue Mermaid!" said Geo.

"Team Umizoomi, you found me!" said the Blue Mermaid.

"Not so fast, Team Umizoomi!" It was Squiddy! "You'll never get past my best invention yet—robot crabs!"

Squiddy opened a box, and soon the robot crabs were crawling all over!

"Look! The crabs are moving in a pattern," said Milli.

"It goes small, big, big! Small, big, big!"

Milli knew how to trap the crabs with her Pattern Power! She made bubbles that were small, big, big, small, big, big, small, big . . .

What comes next, big or small?

195

Squiddy was trapped in a bubble, too! The Blue Mermaid was free!

Squiddy started to cry. "Blue Mermaid, if you leave, my castle will be dark and I'll be scared!"

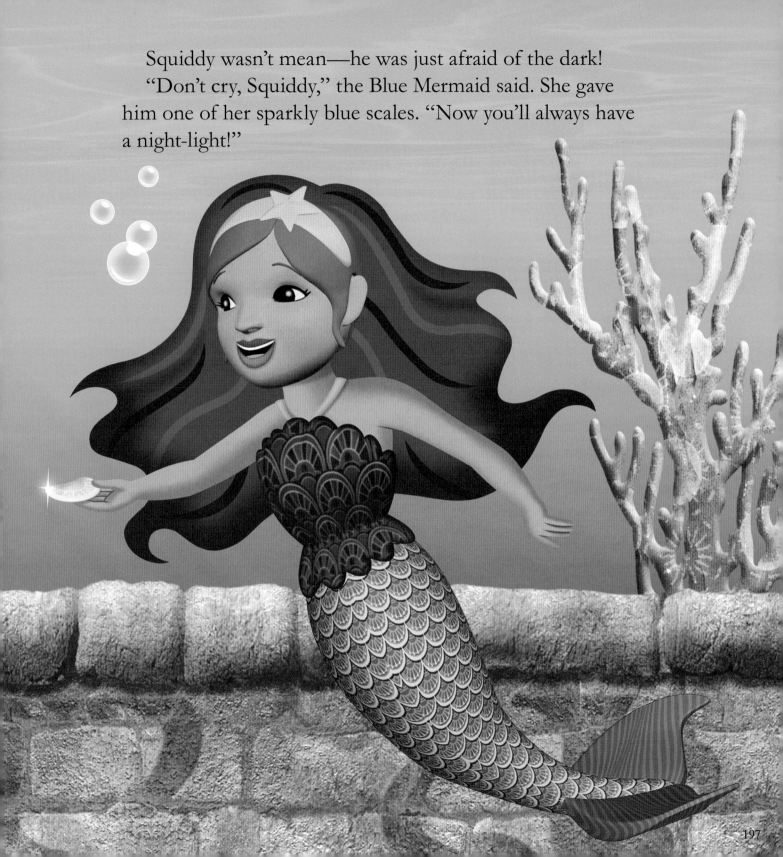

Squiddy wasn't mean—he was just afraid of the dark!
"Don't cry, Squiddy," the Blue Mermaid said. She gave
him one of her sparkly blue scales. "Now you'll always have
a night-light!"

The Blue Mermaid was back where she belonged!
"Thank you, Team Umizoomi!"
2, 4, 6, 8! Everybody Crazy Shake!

UMICAR'S
BIG RACE

It was the day of the big Umi City Car Race. Milli, Geo, and Bot were excited because UmiCar was going to be in the race.

A mean dump truck was going to race, too. He thought
UmiCar was too small to compete, and he laughed at him.
"Don't worry, UmiCar," Milli said. "You're small, but you're

Team Umizoomi fastened their seat belts.

"Come on, UmiCar," shouted Geo.
"Let's race!"

"On your marks! Get set! Go!"
said the announcer.

UmiCar started with a mighty *VROOM!*

UmiCar zoomed down streets and sped around corners.
He passed a tractor, then outraced a taxi.

"UmiCar, you're doing great!" cheered Geo.

UmiCar went over a ramp and flew through the air. He landed with a screech and raced into a park. Team Umizoomi could see a drawbridge ahead.

The drawbridge was up when UmiCar reached it.
The dump truck had made it go up so the other cars couldn't cross
the river!

"How will we get to the other side?" asked Geo.

UmiCar had an idea.

"Leapin' laptops!" said Bot. "There are beach balls in the water. UmiCar thinks we can get across the river by bouncing from ball to ball!"

"The beach balls are in a pattern," Milli said. "They go in this order: small, small, big."

UmiCar started bouncing. Small, small, big. Small, small, big. Small, small . . .

"Oh, no!" said Geo. "The next ball is missing. What should it be?"

Milli knew the next ball needed to be big. She used her Pattern Power to make a big ball so UmiCar could keep bouncing across the river.

UmiCar made it to the other side. Then he lowered the bridge so the other racers could drive across and keep racing. "UmiCar is such a good sport!" said Milli.
ZOOM! UmiCar zipped away.

Suddenly, the dump truck tossed a bucket of soapy water onto the road. The soap made the street super slippery! UmiCar couldn't control his steering wheel. He skidded and slid and crashed to a stop. His steering wheel broke in half!

"Don't worry, team," said Geo. "I can fix the steering wheel with shapes from my Shape Belt. My blueprint says we need a triangle, half a star, and half a ring to build the rest of the

"You did it!" cheered Milli. "Now we can get back in the race!"

UmiCar was almost at the finish line, and there was still one
racer in front of him—the dump truck!

Bot said, "To make UmiCar go faster, we have to count to ten."

The team counted together:
"1, 2, 3, 4, 5, 6, 7, 8, 9, 10!"
UmiCar went faster and faster.
He zipped past the dump truck!

UmiCar crossed the finish line and won the race!
First prize was a big bunch of balloons. UmiCar shared his balloons
with everyone—even the dump truck.

"No one has ever been so nice to me before," said the dump
truck. "I'm very sorry for being mean."

"I feel a celebration coming on!" said Bot.

Team Umizoomi cheered, and the racers honked for UmiCar!

It was Just Because I Love You Day, and Umi Headquarters was very busy. Milli and Geo were using colored paper, scissors, and glue to make cards and gifts for their friends.

"It's a great day to tell your friends you love them," Milli said.

When the cards and gifts were finished, Milli and Geo mailed them.

How many red jars do you see?

Later that day, the Umi Alarm rang. "Geo, a package you sent is stuck at the post office!" Bot announced. "It doesn't have any stamps on it."

"Oh, no! That's the gift Milli and I made for a special friend!" Geo exclaimed. "We have to save it."

"Team Umizoomi, it's time for action!" cheered Milli. The team
jumped into UmiCar and raced to the post office.

"To find the card, we have to know how the post office works," Bot said. "When you put a letter or a package in a mail slot, first it lands in a mail bin.

"Then it goes to the Stamp-Counting Machine. If it doesn't have enough stamps, it drops into the Do Not Deliver Bin.

"If there are enough stamps, it gets put on a mail truck and is delivered."

"Oh, no!" Milli cried. "Our package doesn't have any stamps! We've got to find it before it goes into the Do Not Deliver Bin!"

Team Umizoomi activated their Bouncy Shoes and bounced through a mail slot into the post office.

Team Umizoomi landed in a big pile of letters and packages. "We have to find our special package," Geo said. "Does anyone see a red heart-shaped box?"

"There it is!" Milli exclaimed.

A conveyor belt rushed the special package to the Stamp-Counting Machine. Bot quickly extended his arms and stuck three stamps on the package. "I hope that's enough stamps," he said.

A buzzer buzzed! The Stamp-Counting Machine said the package needed six stamps!

"How many more stamps do we need?" Geo asked. The team counted as Bot added more stamps. "One . . . two . . . three—that makes six!"

The special package was saved from the Do Not Deliver Bin!

How many stamps do you see?

Now Team Umizoomi had to find the right mail truck to deliver it. "We can use the zip code," Milli said. "On every piece of mail, there's a bunch of numbers called a zip code."

Bot added, "Those numbers tell us which neighborhood the mail is going to."

"The zip code on our package is 94110," Milli said. "Where is the truck that matches that zip code?"

"There it is!" Geo cried.

How many orange cones do you see?

Team Umizoomi hopped into the mail truck with their special package. The truck raced through Umi City, and the streets started to look familiar. Suddenly, Bot realized where the package was being delivered—to Umi Headquarters!

Back at Umi Headquarters, Geo said, "The package is for you, Bot, because you're our best robot friend!"

Inside the package were a hat and a card that Milli and Geo had made for Bot. "The hat is green!" Bot exclaimed. "That's my favorite color!"

Milli and Geo hugged Bot. Bot said, "I feel a celebration coming on!"
Everyone danced and hugged some more, and they agreed that it was
an excellent day to tell their friends they love them.

There once was a town named Dead Eye Gulch. Nowadays they call it Bikini Bottom. Back in olden times, it was a lawless place whose citizens lived in fear of a villain named Dead Eye. It was a town that needed a hero.

One day, a mysterious stranger came to town. His name was SpongeBuck, and he was SpongeBob's great-great-great-great-great-great-great-grandfather.

SpongeBuck entered the Krusty Kantina. "Howdy, y'all," he said. "I'm here about the job."

"Great! You're hired," said Mr. Krabs, pinning a gold star to SpongeBuck's shirt. "Hey, everyone, meet the new sheriff."

"But I'm here for the fry cook job!" SpongeBuck said.

"We already gave you the badge, and the law of the west says no take-backs."

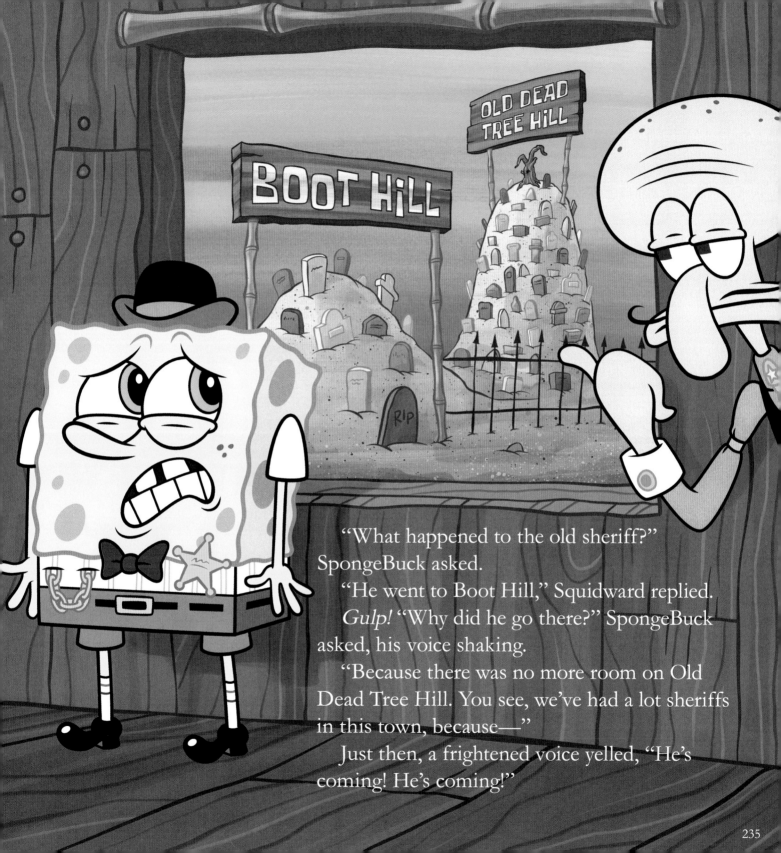

"What happened to the old sheriff?" SpongeBuck asked.

"He went to Boot Hill," Squidward replied.

Gulp! "Why did he go there?" SpongeBuck asked, his voice shaking.

"Because there was no more room on Old Dead Tree Hill. You see, we've had a lot sheriffs in this town, because—"

Just then, a frightened voice yelled, "He's coming! He's coming!"

"Who's coming?" asked SpongeBuck.

"Old Dead Eye!" answered Pecos Patrick. "This was a beautiful town . . . until he rode in and stole everything."

Everyone in the Krusty Kantina had a terrible story about Dead Eye. Mrs. Puff said he made the dancing girls cry. Pecos Patrick said the villain had once stolen his pants.

"Dead Eye has the IOU for my saloon," cried Mr. Krabs. "It comes due at noon. If someone doesn't help us, we'll lose everything we own!"

Everyone went silent as they heard the click-clack of tiny boots enter the Kantina.

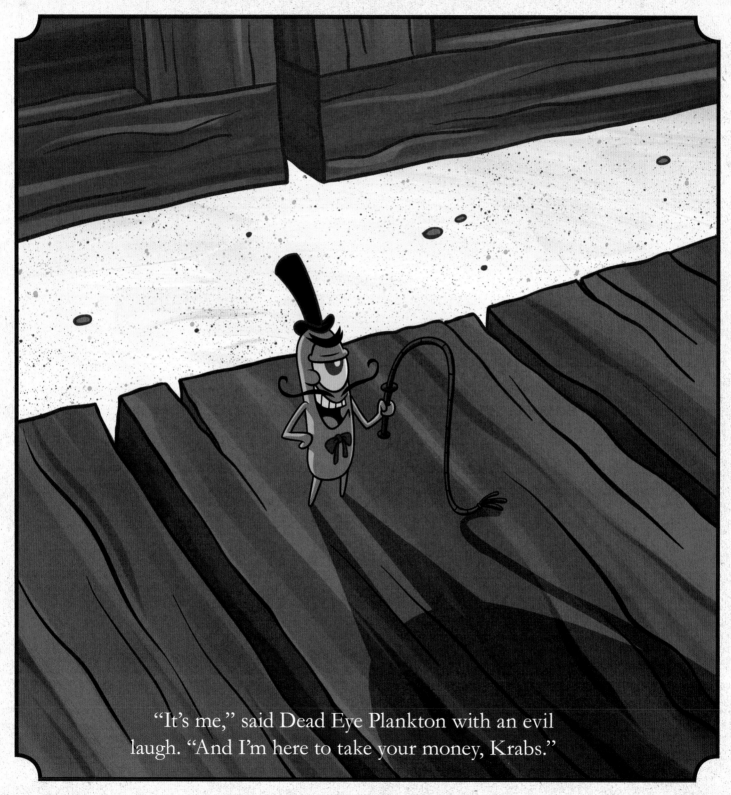

"It's me," said Dead Eye Plankton with an evil laugh. "And I'm here to take your money, Krabs."

"Wait a second," said SpongeBuck. "That's not your money."

"Who are you?" asked Dead Eye.

"I'm the new sheriff," declared SpongeBuck, pointing to his badge.

"Well, I'm a villain, and this town ain't big enough for the both of us. Unless you want to settle this with an Old West–style showdown, I suggest you vamoose. I'll be back at high noon to take the deed to the Krusty Kantina."

The people of Dead Eye Gulch thought the
situation was hopeless. There was no way a silly
sponge could stop that nasty bad guy.

They packed up a stagecoach and headed out of
town. "I've got to leave before I lose all my money,"
Mr. Krabs cried. "My beautiful money!"

They came to a sudden stop. SpongeBuck stood in
the road, blocking the way.

"You can't leave," he said. "If I've learned anything in the twenty minutes I've been here, it's that I love this town. And if we all stand together, we can beat that Dead Eye!"

But no one would stand with SpongeBuck . . . no one except Pecos Patrick.

"In the West, a man can doing anything with the help of his idiot sidekick," said Pecos Patrick. "And that's me!"

The town clock struck noon. It was time for the showdown.

Dead Eye Plankton stood at one end of the dusty street. SpongeBuck was at the other end. They slowly walked toward each other. The people of Dead Eye took cover and watched the action, fearing the worst.

Dead Eye smiled cruelly. SpongeBuck was nervous.
His hands were sweaty. He took another step, and . . .

SpongeBuck stepped on Dead Eye Plankton! The villain was defeated!

Everyone in town ran out from their hiding places and cheered. "Three yeehaws for SpongeBuck!"

"That looks like fun," said Mr. Krabs. "Let me give him a stomp!"

The townspeople went to the Krusty Kantina to celebrate.
Mr. Krabs charged a dollar to step on Dead Eye, and everyone lined up.
"Haven't you people had enough?" Dead Eye groaned.

"Well, Sheriff, you saved the town," said Pecos Patrick.

"Yup. And more importantly, I learned the value of idiot friendship." The two friends clinked glasses and drank their milks in a single gulp.

"I was just thinking," said SpongeBuck. "If I ever have a great-great-great-great-great-great-great-grandson, I hope he's proud of me."

"I'm sure he will be," said Pecos Patrick.

It was a very special day for Mr. Krabs. "SpongeBob, me boy, I have something important to tell you," he said.

"What is it, Mr. Krabs?" SpongeBob asked.

"I've finally found a way to keep Plankton from stealing me secret Krabby Patty formula," Mr. Krabs replied. "I've sent it far, far away, where he'll never be able to find it!"

"That's great, Mr. Krabs!" SpongeBob said. Then he frowned. "But we just ran out of Krabby Patties, and we need the formula to make more!"

"Ah, tartar sauce!" Mr. Krabs grumbled. "The formula's all the way on the opposite side of the ocean!"

"I'll get it, Mr. Krabs," SpongeBob said. "Send me!
I won't let you down."

"This is a very important mission, boy. The formula is in
a safe-deposit box in the ocean's largest and safest bank,
in Way Far-Out Townville," Mr. Krabs explained. He pulled
out a key from his pocket. "This is the key to the box.
Guard it with your life, SpongeBob."

"Aye, aye, sir!" SpongeBob said, determined
to do his best.

Later that day, SpongeBob and Patrick boarded the Oceanic Express to go to Way Far-Out Townville. Little did they know that Plankton was following them.

"Remember, Patrick," SpongeBob said. "This is an important mission. Keep your eyes open for any suspicious characters."

SpongeBob and Patrick walked through the train to the dining car.

"Hey, SpongeBob, does that guy look suspicious to you?" Patrick whispered. "I think he might be spying on us!"

SpongeBob chuckled. Patrick was staring at his own reflection!

"Relax, Pat. I don't think *he* will give us any trouble," SpongeBob replied.

A man walked up to them. "I'm sorry, but the dining car is closed," he said in a snooty way.

"But we haven't even heard the specials yet!" SpongeBob said.

"No! The dining car is over for *you*. You must leave now!" the man snapped.

He grabbed SpongeBob and Patrick and tossed them out of the dining car.

"Well, that was certainly suspicious!" SpongeBob exclaimed. "Patrick, we'll have to find a safe place to store this for the night."

He reached into his pocket for the key, but couldn't find it! "The key! It's gone!" he yelled.

Just then, SpongeBob spotted Plankton. "Plankton, *you* stole the key!" he said.

"I just got here! I couldn't have stolen it . . . yet," Plankton said with an evil grin.

"I don't believe you. Search him, Patrick," SpongeBob ordered.

Patrick lifted Plankton up and shook him upside down. "He's clean," Patrick said.

"Then someone *else* on this train must have stolen the key!" SpongeBob said.

SpongeBob and Patrick called the police and rounded up the suspects.

"I think I know who did it," SpongeBob said. "Mr. Police Chief, I submit to you the nanny! Search this baby's diaper and you'll find the key."

The police chief searched—and found a stolen diamond in the baby's diaper!

"Great job, Mr. SquarePants! You nabbed the infamous Jewel Triplets Gang!" the inspector said.

"Hmm, if they didn't do it, then it has to be the butler," said SpongeBob. "The butler always commits the crime! Shake him down!"

When the police chief revealed that the "butler" had been wearing a mask, the cop exclaimed, "It's Oren J. Roughy! He's an international fugitive wanted for stealing more than seventy-five thousand dollars worth of ham sandwiches! Thank you, Mr. SquarePants!"

"You're welcome, but what about the key? I've failed Mr. Krabs!" SpongeBob wailed.

"Don't worry, it'll turn up," Patrick replied as he pulled something out of his pocket and began to pick his teeth with it.

"Patrick, that's the key! Where did you find it?" SpongeBob asked.

"I found it when I was cleaning your shorts earlier," Patrick answered.

"Oh," SpongeBob said sheepishly.

With the key found, SpongeBob and Patrick settled
down for a nap.

"Would you mind scooching over, SpongeBob?"
Patrick asked. "I can't even move my eyebrows."

"I'm trying, Patrick, but it's really cramped. This
isn't exactly Bikini Bottom!" SpongeBob said.

Suddenly, Plankton popped up from under the covers. "Need more room?" he asked, opening the window. "Maybe I can help."

"What a cool view," Patrick said.

"Have a better look," said Plankton. Then he pushed SpongeBob and Patrick right out of the window. "So long. And thanks for the key!"

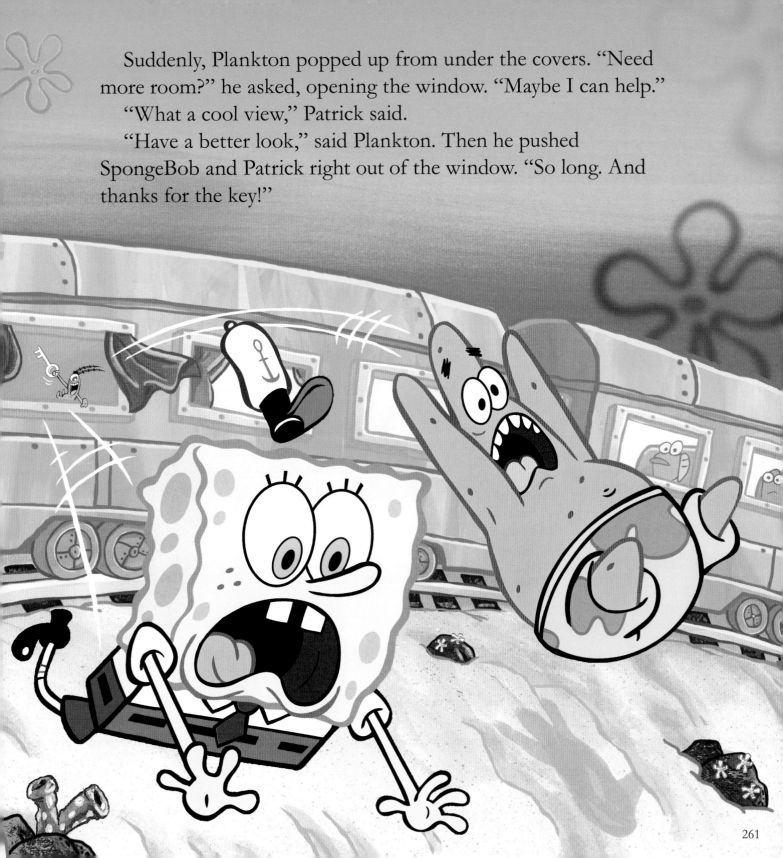

"What are we going to do, SpongeBob?" Patrick asked.

"Follow that train!" SpongeBob said.

They ran after the train until they came to the edge of a cliff. The train pulled away from them and followed the tracks into a canyon below.

"Uh-oh. Now what?" Patrick asked.

"Not to worry, Patrick. I have an idea," SpongeBob said. He grabbed Patrick and jumped off the side of the cliff.

"Ahhhhhhh!" Patrick screamed.

But SpongeBob just smiled as he flopped and flapped—and changed into the shape of a hang glider!

They soon landed safely on the roof of the train.

SpongeBob and Patrick climbed down into the train. They chased Plankton from one car to the next.

"You won't get away with this, Plankton!" said SpongeBob.

Finally, SpongeBob and Patrick chased Plankton all the way to the front of the train.

"All right, Plankton, end of the line!" SpongeBob cried.

"For you, maybe," Plankton replied as he quickly unhitched the engine from the passenger cars.

"Uh-oh, Patrick, we've got a big problem!" SpongeBob said. "We're on a runaway train!"

"Quick, look around. There has to be a way to stop this thing!"
SpongeBob told Patrick.

Patrick stared at the control panel. He found a lever labeled BRAKE.

"Don't worry, SpongeBob, I'll save us!" he said. Patrick grabbed the
lever and jerked it back and forth until it broke! He proudly showed
SpongeBob the broken handle.

"Patrick, you broke the brake!"
SpongeBob cried.

"It told me to," Patrick replied.

The train kept speeding down the tracks,
and SpongeBob and Patrick were helpless to stop it!
It burst through a train station and
looped through the dreaded
Twisted Trestles.

Meanwhile, Plankton sneaked into the Way Far-Out
Townville Bank. He used the key to open the safe-deposit
box. "At last, my day of triumph has come!" he said.

As he picked up the Krabby Patty formula, a voice called
out, "Just a minute, Plankton."

Mr. Krabs stepped out from the shadows. "Did you
honestly think I wouldn't have planned for you?"

Plankton sighed as he handed over the formula. "Just
keeping it warm for you, Krabs."

Suddenly they heard a rumbling sound. *Chugg-a, chugg-a, chugg-a, chugg-a!*

"What's that noise?" Mr. Krabs asked. When he turned to look, Plankton swiped the formula.

"Checkmate, Krabs! I win!" Plankton cried.

All of a sudden, a train smashed through the wall of the bank! SpongeBob and Patrick had arrived just in time. SpongeBob hopped down from the train and took the Krabby Patty formula from Plankton.

"Good job, boy!" Mr. Krabs said. "You saved the day!"

SpongeBob replied proudly, "I refused to fail, sir."

One blustery day, SpongeBob and Patrick were watching the clouds. "That one looks like Sandy," said SpongeBob. "And that one looks like Mr. Krabs."

"Look at that one!" exclaimed Patrick. "It looks like . . . um . . . a cloud!"

Suddenly, something strange and glowing floated overhead.

"It's a haunted houseboat!" shrieked SpongeBob.

But Patrick wasn't convinced. "Nah, it's probably one of those fake haunted houses for babies." Patrick marched up the creaky stairs and went inside. SpongeBob nervously followed him.

"This is *sooo* not scary," Patrick said as he wandered through the dark house.

But it seemed pretty creepy to SpongeBob: doors squeaked open and then closed by themselves, spiders spun webs, and ghostly hands reached out from the darkness.

With a flash of lightning and a roar of thunder, a ghostly pirate captain appeared.

"Who dares trespass on me haunted houseboat?" he bellowed.

SpongeBob and Patrick cowered. "We do," SpongeBob said. "Why have you come to Bikini Bottom, Mr. Pirate, sir?"

Usually, I come to a town to terrify the people and enslave their souls in eternal torment!" the ghost captain boomed. "But this time, my boat's engine is broken. It needs a new gasket.

"Maybe you two could get a new gasket for the engine?" the ghost captain said. "And to make sure you return, I'll keep your souls for a deposit."

He poured SpongeBob's and Patrick's souls into two old soda bottles.

Then the ghost captain opened his treasure chest and handed SpongeBob a gold doubloon. "This will help you buy a new gasket. If you aren't back in twenty-four hours, your souls will become part of my ghastly crew forever!"

SpongeBob and Patrick ran screaming from the haunted houseboat all the way to the Krusty Krab. They burst through the doors and told Mr. Krabs about the ghost, the broken engine, the gold coin, and the treasure chest.

"Did you say *gold*?" asked Mr. Krabs with a sly smile.

Mr. Krabs marched outside and took a gasket from a car. When he returned, he said, "Let's go see this ghost fella. I'll catch him and take all his gold!"

"Great!" said Sandy. "I've been looking for an excuse to use my newfangled paranormal-critter-detector-catcher gizmo!"

The ghost hunters returned to the creepy old houseboat. They
tiptoed across the creaky floors and searched the shadowy rooms.
SpongeBob cried, "Look! Gold doubloons!"

Mr. Krabs giggled with joy as he ran to the treasure chest and hugged it. He quickly shoved clawfuls of coins into bags and threw them to Patrick and Squidward.

"Let's get while the getting's good," Mr. Krabs said with a chuckle.

The pirate ghost materialized with a flash of lightning.

"Who dares to take me gold?" he bellowed.

"It's just us," SpongeBob said. "We brought you a gasket for your engine. I was hoping you'd give me and Patrick our souls back now."

"*Arrgh*, a deal is a deal," the ghost captain said. SpongeBob handed
the gasket to a ghostly crew member, who floated off to fix the engine.

The ghost captain poured a bottle of orange fluid into SpongeBob's head. He threw another bottle to Patrick, who dropped it. The bottle broke, and Patrick quickly started licking up the spill.

"Don't worry," the ghost captain said. "You can't really take a person's soul. That's just old orange soda."

"I *thought* my soul tasted a little flat," Patrick said.

Meanwhile, Mr. Krabs was trying to sneak away with the
gold. As he slowly pulled open a door, it let out a long creak.
The ghost captain heard it and swooped after him,
shouting, "No one gets away with me gold!"

Suddenly, the door swung all the way open. Mr. Krabs, Squidward, and Patrick were sucked into a strange black emptiness with no up and no down.

"And no one escapes the Void!" the
ghost captain said with an evil laugh.

Back on the houseboat, Sandy jumped into action.
"Hey, coffin breath—you'll let my friends out of there
if you know what's good for ya!"

Energy bolts flew from her ghost catcher and pulled
Mr. Krabs, Squidward, and Patrick out of the Void.

As Mr. Krabs and the ghost captain began to fight over the gold, SpongeBob made a discovery.

"Hey, this gold belongs to the Flying Dutchman, the most feared pirate ghost in the sea! His name and phone number are on this chest."

"I was part of his crew," the ghost captain said. "I took his gold a long time ago, but he'll never find me."

Boom! A cannonball crashed through the door and revealed . . . the Flying Dutchman!

"You treacherous sea devils!" he growled. "Give me back me gold, or I'll make you all part of me cursed crew!"

"This might be a good time to leave," SpongeBob whispered. He dragged Mr. Krabs out the door, and his friends followed.

"I wonder how the Dutchman found his gold after all these years," Sandy said.

"I couldn't resist my civic duty," SpongeBob said. "You should always report stolen property to the authorities—especially haunted treasure."

SpongeBob and Patrick hurried through Bikini Bottom to get to Medieval Moments restaurant.

"C'mon, Patrick, it's almost time for the joust!" said SpongeBob. The two friends stood before the entrance.

A booming voice played over the castle's speakers. "You're just twenty wizard's paces away from swords, sorcery, and bad hygiene!"

The restaurant's stadium was packed with a cheering audience. The
medieval king cleared his throat and spoke into a microphone. "By
royal decree, I ask that two people come forth for the royal joust!"

SpongeBob and Patrick waved their hands wildly. "Over here! Pick
us!" they cried. The king called them into the arena.

"I can't believe we'll be watching the royal joust from so close up!"
SpongeBob said.

"You are not watching the joust," an attendant remarked. "You are
in the joust!"

SpongeBob and Patrick nervously climbed onto their sea horses. "Mr. Sea Horse, sir . . . you're gentle on beginners, aren't you?" SpongeBob whispered. Suddenly, both sea horses bucked up into the air.

"SpongeBob, HELP!" yelled Patrick. The boys flew off the sea horses and crashed through the wall!

PLOP! SpongeBob and Patrick hit the ground.

"Look, Patrick!" said SpongeBob. An army of knights was charging toward them. "Some employees from the restaurant are coming to help us!"

"Arrest them for committing the act of witchcraft by falling from the sky!" ordered one of the knights. "Taketh them to jail!"

"Wow, they really go the extra mile here!" SpongeBob said.

In the royal dungeon, SpongeBob and Patrick heard a familiar sound. It was bad clarinet playing!

"Squidward? What are you doing here?" asked SpongeBob.

"My name is Squidly!" said the prisoner. "I was the royal fool until I told a bad joke and the king locked me up!"

"We really *are* in medieval times!" said SpongeBob. "We must have gone back to the past!"

Suddenly, they felt a rumble in the dungeon. "That is the evil
wizard's dragon sent to destroy the king's village," explained Squidly.
Then a guard came and took them all to King Krabs.
"Mr. Krabs?" asked SpongeBob.

"I am the feared ruler of this kingdom!" said the king. "I know you have been sent by Planktonamor to destroy me! It is time for your punishment. Off with their heads!"

"Aahh!" cried SpongeBob and Patrick.

"Wait, Father! Spare them!" the king's daughter, Princess Pearl, begged. "Hast thou forgotten the famous prophecy?"

"What prophecy?" asked King Krabs.

Pearl told the story about how two brave knights
were supposed to fall from the sky and slay the dragon
of Planktonamor, the evil one-eyed wizard!

"Don't you see? These strangers have been sent to
rescue us!" Pearl cried.

Suddenly, a huge jellyfish dragon crashed through the castle and grabbed Princess Pearl!

"Help me, Father!" screamed Princess Pearl.

"Let go of her, you overgrown amoeba!" shouted King Krabs.

"The evil Planktonamor's dragon has taken Pearl!" cried King Krabs. "And he won't return her until I give him my kingdom!"

"Bummer," said Patrick.

"You two brave knights have been chosen to rescue Princess Pearl!" ordered King Krabs.

"We're ready, Your Majesty!" said SpongeBob.

"And take my fool, Squidly, with you!" added the king.

The trio first stopped at the local blacksmith to get proper armor for the trip.

"We have a long journey ahead of us," said Squidly.

SpongeBob reached inside his pocket and pulled out a brown bag. "I always carry some delicious Krabby Patties with me," he said. "After we rescue the princess, we'll have a snack."

"Ooooh!" said Patrick.

Soon SpongeBob, Patrick, and Squidly came face to face with the fearsome dark knight who guarded the bridge to Planktonamor's castle.

"None shall pass!" the dark knight boomed.

"But we have to pass, oh scary knight who looks a lot like my friend Sandy," said SpongeBob. "The king has sent us to rescue the fair Princess Pearl from the evil Planktonamor!"

"Thou will haveth to get past me first!" said the dark knight.

"Hi-yah!" shouted SpongeBob as he karate-chopped her weapon in half.

"What is this strange new fighting technique?" asked the dark knight.

"It is called *karate*," said SpongeBob.

"It pleases me!" said the dark knight. The two fought in a series of karate battles, and SpongeBob won.

"Since you have bested me in battle and spared my life, I shall let you all cross, and I shall accompany you on your quest!" said the dark knight.

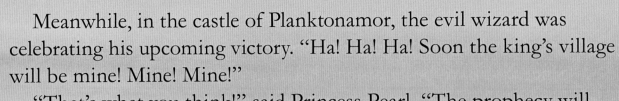

Meanwhile, in the castle of Planktonamor, the evil wizard was celebrating his upcoming victory. "Ha! Ha! Ha! Soon the king's village will be mine! Mine! Mine!"

"That's what you think!" said Princess Pearl. "The prophecy will come true! My rescuers will save me!"

The dark knight helped SpongeBob, Patrick, and Squidly get past the evil wizard's guards. They climbed up the tower stairs to rescue Princess Pearl.

"Hang on, Princess Pearl! We're coming to help you!" yelled SpongeBob.

"And then we'll eat!" added Patrick.

SpongeBob was determined to stop Planktonamor.
"Unhand her, you fiend!" he yelled.

Planktonamor laughed. "Why don't you maketh me?"

"I shalleth!" replied SpongeBob.

"Destroyeth them, dragon!"
ordered Planktonamor.

The giant jellyfish dragon swooped around the castle zapping the intruders.

"I'm afraid this is the end, Patrick!" SpongeBob said, sobbing.

"But I want my Krabby Patty!" cried Patrick.

"Good idea!" said SpongeBob, pulling them out.

Just as Patrick was about to take a bite, the dragon took the food with its tentacle!

"Look! The dragon's eating the Krabby Patty!" exclaimed SpongeBob.

"Hey, dragon!" yelled Planktonamor. "What part of 'destroyeth' dost thou not understand?"

The giant dragon ignored its master and happily kept munching away.

"We defeated the dragon!" shouted SpongeBob.

"Curses!" said Planktonamor. "Foiled by a Krabby Patty!"

King Krabs threw a royal parade for the new heroes. "For your reward, brave knights, I shall give you my two prize sea horses!" said King Krabs.

SpongeBob and Patrick got on the sea horses and began to ride. Suddenly, the horses lost control, and SpongeBob and Patrick were bucked up into the sky!

"Hey! Wake up, you guys!" said the Medieval Moments waiter. "You fell on your heads and got knocked out!"

"Wow, Pat!" said SpongeBob. "That was some dream!"

"So, can we eat now?" asked Patrick.